·⁺Pet Talent Show!⁺·

Adapted by Mickie Matheis
Based on the teleplay "Untamed Talent" by Dustin Ferrer
Illustrated by Cartobaleno

🔖 A GOLDEN BOOK • NEW YORK

T#: 521481
randomhousekids.com
ISBN 978-1-5247-2060-5
Printed in the United States of America
10 9 8 7 6 5 4 3 2 1

P9-CFS-214

It was an exciting day in Zahramay Falls—the amazing Pet Talent Show was just about to start!

Shimmer, Shine, and Leah peeked out from behind the curtain. They couldn't wait to watch their furry friends perform. Plus, the winning pet would get one wish granted by Princess Samira herself!

A few minutes later, Zeta watched her pet dragon, Nazboo, practice his dance moves. As usual, the tricky sorceress was up to no good!

"When we win, you're going to wish for a gem that will make me the most powerful person in Zahramay Falls!" Zeta reminded her pet.

The little dragon nodded and went back to dancing.

It was showtime! The first pet to perform was Leah's fox, Parisa. Using her tail and paws, Parisa painted a magical masterpiece . . . and then disappeared into it!

Princess Samira and the genie audience cheered. They loved it!

Zeta was worried. "That act was better than I thought it would be." She gave Nazboo a grin. "Come on. Let's go cheat!"

Next up was Shine's pet tiger, Nahal.

"Nahal is going to play a tiger tune on her keyboard!" Shine announced. The genie snapped her fingers, and a giant keyboard appeared. "Go get 'em, tiger!"

Nahal pounced on the keys and played
"Mary Had a Little Lamb."

"This act is good, too," Zeta said. "There must be something I can do to ruin it."

Nazboo stood nearby, playing with a feather. That gave Zeta an idea. She cast a spell on the feather and sent it floating out onstage to distract the tiger cub.

Sure enough, Nahal spotted the feather and started to chase it! She raced up and down the giant keyboard, swatting at the floating feather.

But things didn't go quite the way Zeta had hoped. With every step Nahal took, her song sounded better and better. The crowd applauded wildly!

"Ugh! I can't believe my plan backfired!" Zeta moaned. "If we want to win this contest, we have to make sure the next act is terrible!"

It was time for Shimmer's pet monkey, Tala, to perform.

"She's going to do a super-super-super-cute dance," Shimmer told the audience.

Zeta was outraged. "They're doing a dance? But *we're* doing a dance! Those genies have gone too far!"

"Let's see if that monkey can dance on slippery ice," the sneaky sorceress muttered. *"Slide and slip, fall and spin. Turn to ice so we can win!"* she chanted.

Suddenly, the stage floor turned into a sheet of ice!

But instead of falling, Tala began to glide and leap like a graceful ice-skater. Her final move was to carve a silly monkey face into the ice!

The audience was amazed! And another one of Zeta's plans had backfired.

Just then, Nazboo's name was called. It was Zeta's
pet's turn to perform!

Zeta had to think fast. Maybe Nazboo could still
win if his act had some extra-special flair. Zeta quickly
cast a spell on the props in the dressing room.

She held her breath as Nazboo began. The dragon's first steps were perfect—until one of the enchanted props flew across the stage!

Nazboo wobbled and tripped as the enchanted props tumbled around the theater. Curtains ripped. Lights fell. Pillars tipped over. Pets ran from the runaway props.

It was chaos!

Nazboo acted fast! Using a curtain cord, the little dragon swung around and saved all the other pets from the flying props. He delivered each pet safely to its owner.

Then he ran toward Princess Samira. A giant pillar was about to topple over onto the princess and her pet peacock, Roya! Nazboo pushed their seats out of the way just as the entire set came crashing down.

Nazboo had saved the princess and the peacock!

Zeta stepped onto the stage and looked apologetically at the audience. "Sorry about the mess," she said sadly. She picked up Nazboo and was just about to leave when Princess Samira appeared in a poof of sparkles.

"Hold on, Zeta," the princess said sweetly. "I have to announce the **winner**."

"Roya and I thought all the acts were *Zahramazing*!" the princess said to the audience. "But there was one performer who was talented *and* brave. The winner of the Pet Talent Show is . . . NAZBOO!"
The genies and their pets clapped and cheered.

Zeta tried not to look surprised. "Well, of course I knew Nazboo would win," she said.

"For his prize, he would like to $wish$ for a gem."

"And which one would you like?" the princess asked Nazboo.

The dragon whispered into her ear.

"Wish granted," the princess said with a wave of her magic scepter. There was a small puff of pink smoke, and a large Genie Gem appeared in Nazboo's claws. The little dragon was overjoyed.

Zeta immediately snatched it from him.
"Finally! This gem will make me the most
powerful person in Zahramay Falls!"

She cackled gleefully and hugged the gem
close. To her surprise, it let out a loud squeak!
Zeta stared at the gem, confused.

She glared at her pet. "Nazboo, did you wish for a squeaky-toy gem?"

Nazboo nodded.

Zeta groaned. "All that work for a squeaky toy!"

But the other pets thought Nazboo's
pick was just perfect.
Thanks to Nazboo, the Pet Talent Show
ended with a bang—and a squeak!